High Tech Overload

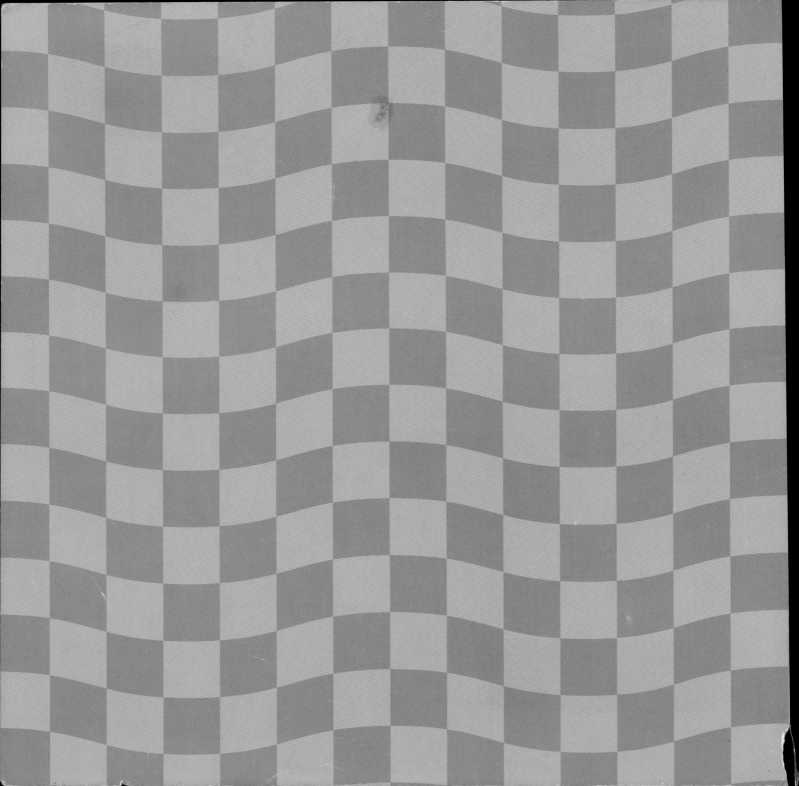

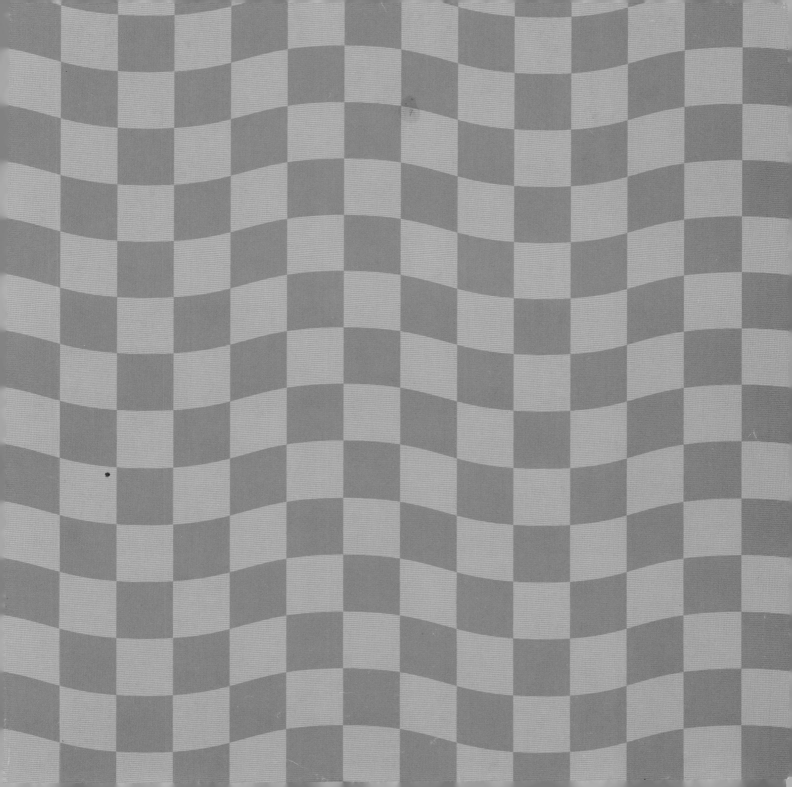

First published in Great Britain by HarperCollins Children's Books in 2011
10 9 8 7 6 5 4 3 2 1
ISBN: 978-0-00-736607-1
© Chapman Entertainment Limited & David Jenkins 2011

Based on the television series, Roary the Racing Car and the original script,
High Tech Overload, by Wayne Jackman. Adapted for this publication by Mandy Archer.

The HarperCollins website address is www.harpercollins.co.uk

Visit Roary at www.roarytheracingcar.com

Printed and bound in China.

High Tech Overload

HarperCollins *Children's Books*

It was an exciting morning for Big Chris. An up-to-the-minute mechanic's computer had arrived in the post.

"Happy days!" he chuckled, flipping open the lid.

Roary peeped over from his parking bay. "What is it, Big Chris?"

"When you cars are racing round the track, this gizmo will tell me what's wrong with you," grinned the chief mechanic, heading out the door. "What a beauty!"

"Why does Big Chris need a machine to find out what's wrong with us?" wondered Cici. "Normally we just tell him!"

"At least we get to race while he tries it out," remarked Maxi.

The cars revved their engines, then drove out to the pit lane. Drifter and Tin Top were out on the track already.

"Wow!" shouted Roary. "Formula fun!"

Drifter and Tin Top were having a wonderful warm-up lap.

"Checking computer for track conditions," said Drifter, slowing down for a mile or two. "Road surface slippery."

"Yee-hah!" yelled Tin Top. "Never mind about your computer, let's race!"

Drifter was so busy listening to his onboard computer, he overshot the bend.

"Whooaaa!"

Tin Top pulled over and laughed. "Maybe you should ditch the high tech stuff and brush up on your steering!"

Drifter wasn't the only one having a few technical hitches.
No matter what he tried, Big Chris couldn't get his new gadget to work.
"WRONG BUTTON," said the gizmo. "CHECK INSTRUCTION MANUAL."
"I'm a mechanic," tutted Big Chris. "I don't need to read the instructions!"

When Drifter and Tin Top had cruised back to the pits, it was time to get the race started. Marsha climbed into the Marshall's tower then waited for all of the cars to line up.

"Ready, Big Chris?" she called.

The mechanic peered into his new laptop.

"Maybe if I press this button here and flick reset…"

"Ahem!" Marsha coughed loudly. "If you're quite ready I'd like to get this race started!"

Big Chris grabbed his gadget and climbed onto Plugger's running board.

"Don't start till I'm in position," he grinned. "I can't wait to put this little baby into practice!"

The cars were soon zooming along the track, skidding round corners and tearing down straights.

Big Chris waited for the team at Carburettor Corner, pressing a switch to set his gizmo into action.

"AND NOW FOR THE WEATHER," said the announcer's voice. "TODAY IT STAYS FINE."

"Spin my spanner!" frowned the mechanic. "It's picking up the local radio now!"

While Big Chris struggled with his new kit, Drifter was determined to make the most of his high tech fittings.

"My computer will help me win this race!" he called. "Switching to nitro boost!"

Blue flames shot out of the street-car's exhaust, sending him speeding round the course.

Drifter easily overtook Tin Top and the rest of the racers. He was rocketing past Roary when a malfunction symbol flashed up on his display board.

"My computer has blown a fuse," he cried. "I'm losing power!"

"Hurry up, Drifter!" called Roary, taking the lead again.

But all Drifter could do was steer off the track. He rolled to a stop in a meadow by the lake.

Over at Carburettor Corner, Big Chris's gizmo was still playing up.

"COME IN CAR TWENTY FIVE, THANK YOU…" said a funny man's voice.

"It's picking up the taxi rank now!" gasped the mechanic. "What's going on?"

Big Chris pointed his binoculars towards Flat Out Forest. This was no time for tinkering – the race cars were coming down the track!

Big Chris quickly turned his gizmo towards the cars. A red light immediately started to flash on the computer's screen.

"WARNING. ROARY. FLAT TYRE," it announced.

"This could be dangerous," said the mechanic. "I'll have to stop them!"

The cars couldn't
understand why Big
Chris was pulling them
off the track.

"Drive slowly back to
the Workshop, Roary,"
he said firmly.
"Wait there till I can fix
that flat tyre."

"But I haven't got a flat tyre!" gasped his number one car.

Big Chris didn't listen.
Instead he fiddled
with a switch on his
super-duper computer.
"Go on son," he said,
waving him on.
"The rest of you can do
a few more laps. I'll test
each of you in turn."

While Big Chris tracked the other cars on his computer, Drifter's circuit boards switched off.

"I have no power left at all," he sighed. "I'll have to wait to get rescued."

The street-car took a look around him. The lake was really rather pretty, but he'd never had the time to notice it before.

"Must always be too busy checking my computer," he smiled.

Back at the Workshop, Roary felt lonely and miserable. He wasn't on his own for long – Maxi, Cici and Tin Top had all been sent back too. "He says I need an oil change!" puffed Maxi. "Mama Mia! I'm fine." Cici lifted her bonnet. "That thing told me I was overheating. Pah!" "Hot diggety dog!" agreed Tin Top. "I got told that my gearbox was gonna strip, but I'm raring to go!"

Marsha marched in, carrying a clipboard. She looked very surprised to find the Silver Hatch team back in their parking bays.

"You're supposed to be racing!" she cried.

"Big Chris's gizmo decided that we all needed fixing," explained Roary.

Marsha put her hands on her hips. "You all look fine to me."

A few minutes later, Big Chris wandered into the Workshop.
He grinned at his friends, then realised that Drifter was missing.
   "He never came past me," panicked the mechanic.
"We'll have to get a search party out there!"
   "Your computer said we were all faulty," sighed Roary.
   Marsha frowned at Big Chris. "If all the cars drive very slowly,
they could help find Drifter."

It was getting dark by the pond, but Drifter didn't mind a bit.

"This is so peaceful," he smiled.

Cro-ak! A little green frog hopped up to say 'hello'.

Drifter was so pleased to see the little fellow, he made up a song.

"I may be high tech, I may be bright," he trilled. "But there's nothing quite like the real things in life."

While Drifter sang to his new friend, the racing cars pulled up nearby.

"Big Chris," said Cici. "Where can he be?"

Roary flashed his headlights. "Can your new magic machine help?"

Big Chris nodded, then pushed some buttons on his gadget.

"It's no use," he moaned. "It's still picking up the radio."

The music wasn't coming from the Big Chris computer, it was drifting over from the side of the track.

"I may be clever and ever so smart," went the tune. "But here Mother Nature's changing my heart!"

"It's Drifter!" cried Big Chris, directing the cars to the lake. "Don't worry, lad, we'll soon have you home."

Everyone was very pleased to get Drifter back to the Workshop. The team had his computer fixed in no time.

"Were you upset when it overloaded?" asked Marsha.

"Only for a while," grinned the street-car. "Then I enjoyed the peace and quiet. Computers are great, but they aren't everything."

Marsha nodded her head. "Maybe that's something Big Chris should learn too."

Just then, the chief mechanic strolled into the Workshop carrying his new gizmo.

"This thing is the bee's knees," he beamed. "Now it's working properly, I'll scan the cars again to prove it!"

Big Chris pressed a big red button. As if by magic, everything went berserk. Lights switched off and on, the ramp clunked up and down and the Workshop doors whizzed out of control!

"WARNING!" blurted the laptop. "BIG CHRIS OUT OF FUEL!" The gadget bleeped loudly then cut out.

"That's it!" decided the chief mechanic. "We're going back to the simple ways from now on."

Roary and his friends all giggled. "Does that mean we can have our race now?"

"Go on then," chuckled Big Chris. "See you on the track."

Name Drifter

Home The Workshop, Silver Hatch

Fastest Lap Time 1:19

Top Speed 185 mph

Favourite Colour Orange

Most Likely to Say

Go Go Nitro Boost!

Least Likely to Say

I'm happy to cruise with the crowd!

www.roarytheracingcar.com

Race to the finish line with these other great Roary books

Build your own Roary

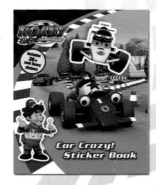
Car Crazy! Sticker Book

Gadget Supercars

Roary races to the rescue

Funny Business

Testing Time

Silver Hatch Pizza

Loada Race Day Truck

Friction Car Assortment

Out now on DVD!

Out NOW!

Rescue and recovery